KU-467-210

For the loveliest Mum and Nan

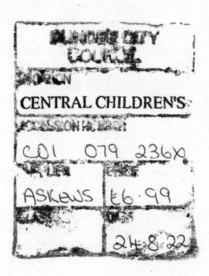

The Hiccupping Dragon

Chapter One

Luma was having the most wonderful dream.

She was jumping up and down on the biggest, bounciest trampoline she had ever seen. Her pet Timir was at her side letting out squeaks and squeals as they bounced higher and higher and higher until Luma could reach out to touch the clouds.

Hic!

Luma looked across at Timir.

'Did you hear that?' she asked.

It happened again.

Hic!

And then again and again.

Luma woke with a sleepy groan. She blinked, confused at first as to what had happened and where she was.

Where had the trampoline gone? Why was her bedroom covered in flowery wallpaper? And what *was* that strange noise?

Luma sat up, a yawn turning into a smile as she looked about.

Of course . . . she and Timir had stayed over at Nani's the night before. They'd had the best evening curled up on the sofa together, watching a film and eating popcorn (Timir ate most of it) and then

Nani had tucked them into bed with not one, not two, but *three* bedtime stories, all about dragons.

Hic!

'Timir? Come out,' Luma said, wiggling her feet. 'There's a funny noise and I don't know where it's coming from.'

Timir usually liked to sleep far under the depths of the covers, pressed up against

Luma's legs, but she couldn't feel him at all.

Luma lifted up the duvet.

Timir was not there.

'Oh,' Luma said, sad to miss out on their morning snuggles. Timir must have woken up early and gone downstairs to see Nani.

Hic!

'There it is again,' Luma said and, with that, she climbed off the bed to investigate.

Luma searched the big wardrobe first, opening the door to a rack full of Nani's old clothes that she had loved to dress up in when she was little.

She knelt down and pushed her hands right to the back of the wardrobe, but there was nothing there – nothing that could make that 'hic' noise anyway.

Luma carried on with her search, looking through the chest of drawers and bedside table. She even checked the window, thinking maybe it wasn't shut properly and squeaking in the wind, but still the noise continued.

There was only one thing for it. She would have to get Timir to help.

Timir had excellent hearing – he could hear Mum opening a packet of biscuits from two rooms away. He would find where the noise was coming from in a flash.

Luma began to walk towards the door when another 'hic' came, this time immediately followed by a 'hup' so loud that Luma stopped in fright.

'Hic . . . hup?' Luma said and then she gasped. 'The noise is a hiccup! That means it must be . . . oh, Timir!'

Chapter Two

Luma rushed back to the bed and lay down on her tummy.

Timir always hid underneath her bed at home when he was afraid and Luma was sure he'd never had the hiccups before. He must be very confused and frightened.

Luma saw a patch of darkness shuffle and then two large round eyes staring worriedly into her own.

'Timir?' she called softly.

'Luma.' Timir's bottom lip wobbled. '*Hiccup!*'

'Don't worry,' Luma said. 'It's just the hiccups. They can't hurt you.'

Timir whimpered. 'I do not like them at all.'

'Why don't you come out and we can try to make them stop?'

Luma sat up and a trembling Timir leapt into her arms.

'Hush now,' she said, stroking his scaly back. 'There are lots of ways to stop the hiccups.'

'There are?' Timir asked.

'Yes,' Luma said, a little bit more confidently than she felt. 'Let me think . . .'

Luma spotted her half-full glass of water on the bedside table and gently set Timir on the carpet. 'You need to drink this in big gulps,' she said, picking up the glass and placing it next to him.

Timir pushed his snout inside the glass . . . '*Hiccup!*'

'Argh!' Timir cried, water blowing from his nostrils.

'Maybe not,' Luma said, putting the glass back. 'Why don't you try holding your breath?'

Timir began to bite at the air. 'Like this?'

Luma giggled. 'No,' she said. 'Watch me.'

Luma sucked in a deep, deep breath, her cheeks puffing out. She held the air in as long as she could and then let it out in a giant whoosh. 'Now you try,' she said.

Timir sucked in a deep breath, his cheeks puffing out and . . . '*Hiccup!*'

'Hmm, that didn't work either,' Luma said. 'There is something else we could try, but . . .'

'What?' Timir asked.

'It means giving you a shock.'

'I don't want a shock,' Timir said. '*Hiccup!*'

'But you do want to stop hiccupping?'

Timir gave a small nod.

'Right, you had better shut your eyes,' Luma said.

Chapter Three

Timir closed one eye.

The other remained wide open, his eyelid flicking up and down to give Luma a suspicious stare.

'You have to close *both* eyes for it to work,' Luma said.

Timir grumbled, but then another hiccup came out and he squeezed his eyes tightly shut.

'And maybe try not to listen either,' Luma said, remembering his super-hearing. She stood up as quietly as she could and tiptoed across the room towards the wardrobe, carefully opening the door.

The hinges squeaked.

Luma glanced back at Timir. His eyes were still closed, but his ears were most definitely twitching.

'No listening!' Luma called and quickly slipped inside.

All was quiet.

Luma counted to one hundred, just like she did when they were playing hide and seek. She reached one hand towards the door and . . .

'*Hiccup!*'

'Timir,' Luma said, opening the door

to find Timir sitting just outside. 'I was supposed to shock you.'

'*Hiccup!*' Timir replied.

Luma sighed. 'I think we had better find Nani.'

Nani was the only other person Timir could be a dragon around *and* the only other person who could hear him speak – when anyone else was about, Timir changed himself into a dog and sounded like he was making some very strange noises!

Timir led the way down the stairs, a hiccup coming out as he bounced on to each step.

They found Nani in the kitchen with a steaming mug of tea in one hand and a pencil held above a puzzle book in the other.

'Good morning.' Nani smiled. 'Did you sleep well?'

'Yes, Nani,' Luma said. 'But Timir has the—'

'*Hiccup!*' Timir hiccupped.

'Ah,' Nani said, her smile disappearing. 'I was wondering when that would happen.'

'What do you mean?' Luma asked. 'Is it normal for a dragon to get the hiccups?'

'It is when their flame is coming,' Nani said.

'Flame?' Luma said. 'That means your fire, Timir.'

Timir whined. 'I do not like fire.'

'I'm not sure I like it either,' Luma said. 'But you are a dragon and all dragons have fire.'

'Yes, but there is no need to worry,' Nani said, reaching down to scratch behind Timir's scaly ears. 'For we have something that will turn Timir's flame completely harmless.'

Luma frowned. 'Do you mean the charm bracelet?'

Nani had given Luma the bracelet just before she found Timir. Each of the five charms contained a little dragon magic of their own.

She already knew that the orb held a scent no dragon could resist – the only thing that had tempted Timir out of hiding on the day they met.

They had also discovered the purpose of the dragon charm when they got lost in the woods during a puppy training class, its flashing lights guiding Luma to Timir.

All that was left was the locket with the little squiggly mark on it, the patterned heart and the odd-looking wing.

None of them looked like they could stop fire.

'This one, Luma,' Nani said, reaching forward to tap the silver locket. 'You see this mark here? It is rather worn away now, but it once was a beautiful engraved flame.'

'But Nani, the locket doesn't open,' Luma said. 'I've tried heaps of times . . . it's broken.'

Chapter Four

'The locket is not broken.' Nani smiled. 'Just waiting for the right time.'

'Will it stop my hiccups?' Timir asked.

Nani shook her head. 'I'm afraid not. You will have to put up with them for a little while longer.'

Timir let out a long, low wail. 'I do not want any flame and I want the hiccups to stop right now ... *hiccup!*'

'When will Timir's flame come?' Luma asked.

'Today or the next day, perhaps.'

'Mum will be back this afternoon and I have to go to school tomorrow. How will I explain Timir's hiccups and what if his flame comes when I'm not there?'

And then the phone rang.

'Ah, I must get that. It will be your auntie calling,' Nani said. 'I won't be long . . . why don't you make breakfast, Luma?'

Timir stared sadly after Nani as she rushed from the kitchen to the telephone in the hall.

'What about jammy toast?' Luma said. 'That will make you feel better.'

Timir's head whipped round to Luma. 'Yummy,' he cooed.

Timir weaved in and out of Luma's feet, hiccupping and licking his lips, as she got everything ready for their breakfast.

'I wonder how the charm works?' Luma said, twisting the locket about as they waited for the toaster. 'What do you think, Timir?'

'Pop!' Timir said, bouncing as the toast popped up.

Luma spooned a generous heap of jam on to each slice.

'More,' Timir said.

Luma put another big spoonful on

Timir's slice. 'But that's it. Otherwise there will be more jam than toast!'

Luma carried their plates into the living room, placing Timir's on the low side table.

Timir rushed forward, biting down on the edge of the toast and . . .

'*Hiccup! Hiccup! Hiccup!*'

'Oh dear,' Luma said as Timir's mouthful of toast sailed into the air.

Timir tried once more.

'*Hiccup!* No!' Timir flumped on his back and wailed. 'My tummy . . . is . . . so . . . empty!'

Chapter Five

Luma put her plate down. She didn't think she should eat when Timir could not.

'Nani will be back soon,' Luma said. 'I'm sure she will know what to do.'

Timir howled.

'Why don't we watch some cartoons?' Luma suggested, grabbing the remote and switching the telly on, but Timir remained on his back, letting out huffs and more hiccups.

Luma hopped off the sofa and peered round the doorway into the hall. Nani was still chattering away with no sign of the call ending.

'What about the garden?' Luma asked, returning to Timir. 'Why don't we go and see the fish in Nani's pond while we wait?'

Timir did not reply.

Luma let out her own sad sigh. It always made her feel terrible when Timir was upset, and what if his flame took days and

days to come? She wasn't sure how Timir would cope with the hiccups for that long – especially not being able to eat!

But then suddenly, Timir rolled on to his front and stood up.

His ears swished forward, his wings lifting and fluttering.

'Is it a squirrel?' Luma asked, looking towards the back door.

Timir, however, turned to look down the hallway to the front door. 'Post,' he whispered.

And then he was gone, changing from a dragon into a dog in a blur.

'Rah!' Luma heard Timir roar, followed by some doggy woofs.

Luma raced into the hallway.

Timir was jumping up and down, barking and biting as the flap of the letterbox lifted.

Nani was standing by Timir's side, the telephone pressed to one ear, as she tried to shoo him away.

'No, Timir!' Luma called, slipping past Nani just in time to whip the letters away from his chomping teeth.

'Well done, Luma,' Nani said, giving Timir a look.

Timir turned around and slunk away.

'I won't be a minute,' Nani said, nodding towards the phone.

Luma followed after Timir.

'That was very cheeky,' she said, as she walked into the living room. 'You know you're not allowed to . . .'

Luma stopped.

Timir was sitting by the low side table, licking his lips, the two plates empty, not even a crumb left.

'No hiccups,' Timir said.

'My jammy toast!'

Timir gave Luma a sheepish grin, shook and was a dragon once more.

'*Hiccup!*'

'How odd,' Luma said. 'I wonder . . . Timir? Turn back into a dog.'

Luma waited as Timir's dragon scales disappeared into his fluffy fur.

'Do you feel a hiccup coming now?'

'No.'

'Change again?'

As soon as his scales reappeared, Timir let out his loudest hiccup yet.

Nani walked into the living room. 'Still hiccupping, Timir?'

'Yes, but actually,' Luma said, 'I think Timir only hiccups when he is a dragon.'

'Ah, did I not tell you that?' Nani asked.

'No,' Luma said.

Timir did a very loud snort.

'Well, it is a good thing too,' Nani said. 'We are due to meet my friend, Flora, at the garden centre soon. We wouldn't have been able to go if Timir was hiccupping as a dog.'

'Ooh!' Luma grinned. 'I love the garden centre. It has the best playground ever.'

'I also have this to give you,' Nani said, walking over to her dresser and pulling out a small silver purse from one of the drawers.

'What is it?' Timir asked. 'I have it?'

'I think you need thumbs to open it, Timir,' Nani said, passing the purse to Luma.

Luma undid the zip and peered inside. 'Three pounds!'

'Your pocket money,' Nani said.

Timir's eyes lit up. 'A new toy for me?'

'Maybe,' Luma said. 'Or a new toy for both of us.'

Nani chuckled. 'Now, why don't you two get ready.'

Chapter Six

Timir bounded up the stairs in front of Luma, spinning in a circle once he'd reached the top and trying to nip his tail.

Luma giggled, greatly relieved to see Timir feeling better.

'Let's brush our teeth first.'

'Teethies!' Timir squealed.

Timir had only got his own toothbrush recently.

Luma's mum had said dogs did not need to have their teeth brushed twice a day – and normally, they did not like it at all. But after Mum had caught Timir 'sharing' Luma's toothbrush one too many times, she had given in.

Luma squirted a large blob of toothpaste on to her red toothbrush and a second big blob on to Timir's blue toothbrush. 'Open wide!'

As soon as she was finished, Timir changed into a dragon.

'Now my dragon teeth,' he said.

'No,' Luma said. 'Remember, you have to be a dog because . . . oh, wait. You haven't hiccupped yet?'

Timir stared down his snout, waiting to see if a hiccup would come out, but his mouth remained closed.

Timir grinned. 'They've gone!'

'I wonder what this means?' Luma said. 'Maybe we should go and tell Nani?'

'After my teeth?' Timir asked.

'I suppose,' Luma said, squeezing

another blob of toothpaste on to Timir's brush.

Luma began to brush Timir's spiky fangs.

'Timir? Why is your nose twitching?' she asked. 'Is the brush tickling?'

Timir made a high, whiny sound and then . . .

A teeny burst of red, orangey fire shot out of Timir's mouth.

'Flame!' Luma exclaimed.

Timir spluttered and groaned, smoke puffing from his nostrils.

And then something very strange

began to happen . . . the foamy splodges of toothpaste began to grow around Timir's snout, doubling and then tripling until Luma could barely see Timir's face.

'What's happening?' Luma cried.

The foam continued to grow, giant bubbles fizzing and frothing and then . . .

Splat!

Luma gasped as the foam exploded, great blobs splattering across the sink and mirror, the bathroom tiles and . . . all over Luma.

'Oh my goodness!' Luma said, wiping toothpaste from her eyes to stare at Timir. 'We need to find Nani, now.'

Luma and Timir raced down the stairs.

'Timir's flame came out,' Luma shouted, jumping the last few steps and skidding round the corner.

Nani rushed out of the kitchen. 'Already? But Timir, you were a dog?'

'I was brushing Timir's dragon teeth,' Luma explained.

'There was bubbling,' Timir said. 'I felt it right in my tummy.'

'And this fiery flame came out – it wasn't hot, though,' Luma said. 'But then Timir's toothpaste foam got bigger and bigger and splattered everywhere.'

'Really? How peculiar,' Nani said. 'Have you checked the charm?'

Luma held up her wrist.

The clasp on the locket was open.

'What's inside?' Timir asked, balancing on his hind legs to see.

Luma slipped the bracelet off and opened the locket fully. 'It's a red, orangey flame . . . no, it looks more green . . . and now blue and purple.'

Nani frowned. 'May I look?'

Luma passed the bracelet to Nani.

Nani's frown deepened as she examined the inside of the locket. 'The colour is changing. I wonder what this means?'

'What colour should it be?' Luma asked.

'Well, like fire, but . . .' Nani paused,

shaking her head. 'I think it should be glowing too.'

'Oh,' Luma said.

'Maybe I'm not remembering correctly,' Nani said. 'Or maybe it is just different for Timir . . . you can never be too sure with these charms.'

'But it must be working if Timir's flame wasn't hot? My hand was right there with the toothbrush and I didn't feel anything at all.'

'Yes, you're right, Luma,' Nani said. 'The charm must be working. Nothing to worry about and now, let's finish getting ready. We need to leave very soon.'

Chapter Seven

Once Luma was dressed and the last splodge of toothpaste wiped away (Timir was most helpful and licked the bathroom tiles clean), they left Nani's house and drove the short distance to the garden centre.

'There's Flora,' Nani said, waving to a tall, grey-haired lady standing by the entrance, as they got out of Nani's car.

'Hello! Hello!' Flora called as they walked closer. 'And who is this?' she asked, bending down to ruffle Timir's fluffy fur.

'This is Timir,' Luma said.

'What a funny-looking thing!' Flora laughed.

'How about we visit the café first?' Nani said, taking Flora's arm and leading her towards the sliding doors. 'Luma and Timir can go to the playground.'

'Sounds lovely.' Flora smiled and then she drew in a large breath and . . . began to talk.

Flora talked to Nani all the way to the café counter, all through ordering their tea and cake and all the time it took for the tea and cake to be prepared.

In fact, Flora did not stop talking until they had found a table outside near the playground and she *had* to stop so she could have a sip of her tea.

Nani just managed to tell Luma they could go, before Flora placed her cup back down.

'Come on, Timir,' Luma said, moving

away. She soon, however, felt a sharp tug on the lead. Timir had positioned himself by Nani's side, as close as possible to  her plate with the large slice of chocolate cake on top.

Luma shook her head. 'Timir?' she said. 'Let's go!'

Timir licked his lips and, with a whine and a sigh, finally turned away, trotting beside Luma until they reached the gate of the play area.

'What should we go on first?' Luma asked.

'Slide!' Timir said, as he watched a little girl go down with a squeal.

Luma and Timir waited patiently in

the line until it was their turn. Luma had
to help Timir scrabble up the ladder. It
was not meant for dog paws.

As soon as Timir got to the top, he slid
down with a loud yowl.

'Again!' Timir said, racing back round
to Luma.

Luma helped him up and this time followed him to slide down herself.

'Again and again!' Timir roared, racing round out of Luma's sight.

There was silence and then . . . a scream! Luma ran.

Timir had pushed himself to the front of the queue and was trying his hardest to get up the ladder himself.

'Sorry,' Luma called, grabbing Timir's lead off the ground and tugging him away. 'Timir, you know you have to wait in line.'

'I do not like to wait,' Timir huffed.

'What about the swings?' Luma said, pointing towards the big tyre swings. 'There is nobody on them.'

Timir woofed and bounded ahead.

Luma sat in the middle of the round rubber tyre and picked Timir up.

'Wheeee!' Timir said as they swung back and forth, his fluffy ears flapping.

'Should we go on the roundabout next or the climbing frame?' Luma asked.

'Roundabout,' Timir said, barely waiting for Luma to slow them down before he leapt from her lap.

Luma jumped off the swing and was just about to bend down to pick up Timir's lead when she froze, her eyes growing large as she caught sight of something she shouldn't be seeing.

'Timir!' she said. 'Your nose! It's changed . . . it's your dragon snout!'

Chapter Eight

Timir's snout began to twitch, just like it had when Luma was brushing his dragon teeth.

Then his mouth dropped open, a small burst of flame shooting out, straight towards the swing they had been sitting on.

Luma gulped as the swing began to twist and turn, see-sawing through the air, higher and higher, before coming to a sudden, creaking stop.

'What was that?' Luma said, glancing about the playground, relieved to see nobody had noticed and even more relieved, when she looked down at Timir, to see his snout had returned to his dog nose.

Timir whimpered. 'Nani.'

'Yes, we need to tell her right now.' Luma nodded. 'Something must be very wrong with the charm.'

Luma grabbed Timir's lead and they ran back through the gate to Nani and Flora's table.

'What good timing,' Flora said. 'We were just about to set off for a browse around the centre.'

'Is everything OK, Luma?' Nani asked.

Luma looked from Nani to Flora.

She was desperate to tell Nani what had happened, but there was no way she could explain with Flora so close.

'We're fine,' Luma sighed.

Flora led them to the planting section first. They spent at least ten minutes staring at a large rack of seeds and rather smelly bulbs as Flora decided between peas or cabbage for her vegetable garden.

Then, it was on to gardening equipment and another boring fifteen minutes while Flora picked a new trowel and spade.

Next, they moved on to the *definitely* smelly fertiliser and plant food aisle and by the time Luma caught sight of the far more exciting aisles ahead, she had calmed right down about Timir and his flame.

After all, the flame hadn't actually

burnt anything so the charm was working and maybe it was just the force of it coming out of Timir's mouth that had made the swing sway?

'Nani, can we go and look for something to spend our pocket money on?' Luma asked, pointing towards the rows of crafts, toys and books. (Flora had stopped talking to take out her reading glasses.) 'You'll be able to see us from here.'

'All right.' Nani nodded. 'But keep checking in.'

Luma grinned and they were off.

'What about a painting set?' Luma suggested, tugging one off the rack and turning it over to see the price. 'No, too expensive,' she said, putting it back.

They wandered further down, weaving in and out of a few other customers, until

Timir stopped to sniff at the pots of clay.

'Can I eat this?' he asked, giving the lid a lick.

'No, that is *not* for eating,' Luma said, moving them on quickly.

They reached the end of the aisle and turned down the next.

'Yo-yo!' Timir squealed, the lead flying out of Luma's hand as he galloped down the aisle.

Luma did not say anything. She really did not want a yo-yo.

And then she spotted a large circular rack, opposite where Timir was nosing inside a box.

'Teddies!' Luma called, running towards them.

✶ ✷ ✶

Chapter Nine

There were bunnies and unicorns, dinosaurs and llamas, butterflies, flamingos and even dragons!

Luma reached for the smallest bunny. 'Look, Timir! It's three pounds exactly.'

'Rah!' she heard Timir roar.

Luma turned around.

Timir was lying on his back, all four paws in the air as he tossed a bright blue yo-yo about.

'Timir, I don't think . . .'

And then the yo-yo clattered to the ground.

Timir twisted on to his tummy and stood up, his nose now his dragon snout

and his ears no longer fluffy, but scaly as well.

Timir rushed towards Luma, nostrils frantically twitching and his cheeks growing rounder and rounder as he tried to hold the flame in.

But it was no good . . .

Whoosh!

The teddies flew.

Left and right and up and down.

A llama sailed past Luma's shoulder, a bright pink sparkly unicorn bumping her on the head.

'Oh no!' Luma said, staring about at the chaos.

'Is my nose dragon?' Timir asked, reaching a fluffy paw up.

'Not any more,' Luma said. 'But, Timir . . . your ears changed too!'

'I need Nani,' Timir cried, trotting towards a gap in the aisles where they could see Nani holding up a bottle of plant food, Flora squinting as she read the label on the back.

'Yes,' Luma agreed. 'We absolutely need to tell Nani this time and probably go straight home . . . first, though, I think we should tidy up.'

Luma and Timir got to work, Luma gathering the teddies that had fallen on to the shelves and Timir picking up the teddies from the floor.

Once the last teddy had been placed on the stand, Luma stood back and studied the display.

'It doesn't look quite as it did before,' Luma said, noticing most of the teddies Timir had placed back were either upside down or sideways – some even looking a little bit damp from his mouth.

And then they heard Nani calling their names.

'What about my yo-yo?' Timir asked, with a whine towards the bright blue yo-yo still on the floor.

Luma picked it up and placed it back in its box. 'I think we should talk to Nani first.'

Except when they reached Nani's side, Flora was *still* chatting away.

'Nani,' Luma whispered.

Nani did not hear.

'Nani!' Luma said louder.

Flora looked down at her. 'Luma, dear, I was talking . . . now, how about we look at the indoor plants? I could do with a new pot for my orchid.'

Flora turned away, tapping Nani's arm as she leant in to continue whatever conversation they had been having.

Luma and Timir looked at each other and sighed.

Soon, they were walking among rows and rows of green leafy plants.

'What are they?' Timir said, drifting towards a table crammed with little cacti.

'I wouldn't sniff those,' Luma said.

'Not sniffing, just looking,' Timir said, standing on his hind legs and propping his front paws on the table. 'So pretty,' he cooed, leaning closer and closer and . . . 'Ow! It bit me!'

Timir turned to Luma, his eyes filling with tears.

'Timir!' Luma said. 'Your nose has changed and your ears and . . . your claws!'

And then Timir's mouth dropped open, his flame soaring right towards Luma!

Chapter Ten

Luma fell backwards with a crash.

'No!' Timir howled, jumping on top of Luma's tummy.

Luma groaned, just able to make out Timir was completely a dog again through his worried licks.

'Are you all right?' she heard Nani call. 'What happened?'

Timir hopped off, revealing a worried Nani and Flora.

'I . . . um, tripped,' Luma said, standing up.

'But what have you done to your clothes?' Flora frowned.

Luma looked down at herself and gulped.

Her T-shirt and jeans were back to front!

Luma looked at Nani.

'Ah,' Nani said. 'Maybe we should—'

'Now, I must have a little browse outside,' Flora said. 'I need a new hanging basket for my front door.'

'You go on ahead,' Nani said. 'We won't be a minute.'

As soon as Flora disappeared through the sliding doors, Nani turned to Luma and Timir.

'What is going on?' Nani asked.

'It's Timir,' Luma said. 'His flame keeps coming out.'

'But he's a dog,' Nani said.

'Parts of him keep changing,' Luma explained. 'First his nose, then his ears and this time, his paws as well.'

'I can't stop it, Nani,' Timir said, his bottom lip wobbling.

'But why are your clothes the wrong way round?' Nani asked.

'It's the flame,' Luma said. 'Strange things happen to whatever it hits . . . first the swing swaying all over the place and then the teddies from the display flying in the air.'

'Oh my,' Nani said. 'What about the charm?'

Luma held up her wrist and opened the locket. 'Still changing colour.'

'And not glowing?' Nani asked.

Luma shook her head.

'We need to go home right now and work out what is wrong,' Nani said. 'I will catch up to Flora and let her know.'

'But my yo-yo, Nani?' Timir said as they followed Nani outside. 'And Luma's bunny teddy?'

'I think we may have to come another time,' Nani said. 'You two wait here. I won't be long.'

Chapter Eleven

They waited and waited . . . and waited.

'Where is Nani?' Luma said, hopping up and down and trying to see over the rack of plants. 'Flora must be chatting again.'

And then a garden centre lady appeared behind them, a long green hose in her hand.

'Ooh,' Timir said, trotting towards her. Timir loved chasing and trying to bite the water from their hose at home.

'I don't think that's a good idea,' Luma said, tugging Timir to the side as the lady began to water the plants next to them.

Timir's shoulders flumped.

Luma felt dreadful. What a terrible day Timir had been having, first with his hiccups, then his flame causing chaos and now they wouldn't even be able to spend their pocket money!

'What about that puddle?' Luma said, as the lady moved further ahead. 'You could stomp in it while we wait for Nani?'

Timir grinned, leaping forward and landing right in the middle of the puddle with a splash.

Luma giggled, pleased to have cheered Timir up for now. She was just thinking of joining him when Timir spun towards her.

'Luma . . .'

Timir's nose, ears and paws were once again his dragon snout, ears and claws and, worse, Luma could see the tips of his spiky spines all along his back and tail, poking out from his fluffy dog fur.

And then a burst of flame, bigger than all those before, poured out towards Luma.

Luma quickly dodged out of the way.

'Phew!' she said. 'That was lucky.'

But Timir was staring above her.

Luma turned around.

The garden centre lady was at the end of the aisle, wrestling with the hose as it spun wildly out of control.

There was a loud scream.

The hose dropped to the ground.

And then Nani appeared with a very wet Flora at her side.

'Well I never!' Flora scowled, wiping the water from her face and glaring at the garden centre lady.

Nani was silent.

Her eyes were fixed on Timir and she looked very worried indeed.

Chapter Twelve

'Timir!' Luma gasped. 'You haven't changed back at all!'

Luma looked up.

Nani and Flora were walking towards them.

'Quick, hide behind my legs or Flora will see you,' Luma said.

Timir scooted behind Luma just in time.

'I can't believe it! Utterly terrible luck!' Flora said as she reached them. 'And now we have to cut our visit short . . .'

Flora turned to give the garden centre lady another glare and, after a hasty goodbye, was gone.

'Oh dear, oh dear,' Nani said as she watched Flora walk away.

'Um . . . Nani,' Luma said, tugging on her arm and pointing at Timir.

Timir's horns had appeared either side of his scaly ears.

'Ah!' Nani exclaimed as a burst of flame hit the pots in front of them.

The plants inside the pots lifted up,

jiggling in the air, before banging down.

'Take off your jumper, Luma,' Nani said. 'We need to cover Timir up and get to the car as quickly as possible.'

Luma pulled her jumper over her head and tied it around Timir's back and then they were rushing back inside the centre.

'Luma!' Timir cried.

Luma looked down.

'Nani!' she called. 'Timir's fur has gone and . . .'

A jet of flame hit a row of neatly stacked pillows upending them on to the floor.

'Pick Timir up now and cover him completely if you can,' Nani said. 'Let's go!'

They carried on, Luma running with Timir in her arms as Nani led the way.

Luma felt Timir begin to tremble under her jumper.

'Just a little longer,' she whispered, finally seeing the exit in the distance.

There was, however, a large obstacle between them and outside.

Long, twisting queues of customers waited at the tills.

Luma felt Timir's trembles turn to rumbles and quakes.

'Nani? What will we do? I don't think Timir can hold on much more.'

'Run, Luma,' Nani said. 'I'll be right behind you.'

Luma sprinted ahead, dodging trolleys, skidding between whole families and nearly bumping into a rack of garden statues, but finally, the way was clear.

Luma burst through the doors, skidding to a stop to catch her breath.

'We made it, Timir,' Luma panted, looking back for Nani making her way through the crowd towards them.

Luma uncovered Timir's head.

Timir's eyes were tightly shut, his brow creased and his snout . . . his snout was furiously twitching.

'Argh!' Luma cried as flame whizzed past, hitting the line of shopping trolleys and sending them tumbling and crashing backwards.

There were loud gasps and shrieks and shouts of 'What was that?!'

Nani appeared at their side. 'Come on,' she said. 'The quicker we leave the better.'

They hurried to the car, Nani opening the back door and ushering Luma and Timir inside.

Luma pulled her jumper off Timir.

'Oh my goodness!'

Timir was completely dragon, not one trace of his fluffy fur left.

'Luum . . .' He tried to speak, but as soon as he opened his mouth, flame seeped out.

Chapter Thirteen

Nani quickly settled into the driver's seat and started the car.

'There's a blanket next to you . . . best keep Timir covered up,' Nani called back to them as they drove off. 'Thank goodness no one saw him at the centre.'

'Why is this happening, Nani?' Luma said, shaking out the blanket and wrapping it round Timir. 'What's wrong with the charm?'

'I'm not sure,' Nani said. 'But we will be home very soon . . . oh dear!'

Flame whooshed between the two front seats, spreading across the windscreen.

The wipers switched on, scraping wildly back and forth.

'Timir?' Nani said, switching them off. 'Try and point your nose down if you can.'

Timir tried his best to control his flame, just as Luma tried her best to keep him covered up, but every few seconds another blast rocketed out, the force of it causing Timir to jolt and jump, the blanket sliding off his back and his flame . . . his flame hitting everything in sight.

By the time they arrived at Nani's house, Luma and Nani's hair was standing on end.

The contents of Nani's handbag bobbed in the air alongside them, lipstick smeared across the windows and loose coins and cough sweets pinging off the car seats.

The radio was blaring.

The windscreen wipers were once again frantically wiping.

The car lights, both inside and out, were flashing and flashing.

'Urgh,' Luma said, as she opened the car door and carried a quivering Timir out. 'That was terrible.'

'Yes,' Nani agreed, trying to flatten her hair as she unlocked the front door.

'What should we do now?' Luma asked, jumping back as the two heavy plant pots either side of the front door tipped over.

'Let's get inside first,' Nani said, swinging the door open and ushering them in.

Luma stepped into the hall just as Timir let out another blast of flame.

The pictures on the wall spun, the coats zipping themselves up on their pegs.

'Or maybe take Timir straight out into the garden,' Nani said.

Luma walked quickly through the living room to the back door . . . not fast enough, however, for the books that fell  off Nani's bookcase, or the cushions that leapt off the sofa, or the curtains that tied themselves into knots.

'You two go,' Nani said, unlocking the door for them. 'I'll just put myself to rights and be out shortly.'

Luma stepped outside.

'Where now, Timir?' Luma asked, but Timir still could not answer.

Luma bit her lip as she watched his flame continue to pour out, spreading over Nani's lawn, ripping out daisies and chunks of grass.

She wasn't sure there was anywhere safe for Timir's flame.

Timir, however, was straining against her.

'What is it?' Luma asked.

Timir tugged harder.

'Should I put you down?'

Luma knelt on the grass and Timir dashed away to the gate that separated Nani and Luma's gardens.

Luma ran to catch up. 'Through here?'

Timir nodded.

As soon as Luma undid the latch on the gate, Timir shot off towards the tall, tall trees.

Chapter Fourteen

'Timir!' Luma called. 'What are you doing?'

Timir disappeared into the trees.

Luma dropped down to her hands and knees and shuffled through the overgrown shrubs and tree trunks.

Timir was huddled in the exact same spot she'd found him the first day they had met.

Luma rushed towards him, but Timir spun away as another burst of flame came out, rattling the trees above them.

'What will we do?' Luma cried. 'Why is the charm not working?'

Luma let out an angry roar, ripping the bracelet off her wrist and flinging it away . . . just as Timir turned towards her, his mouth open as flame shot out, hitting the bracelet.

The bracelet froze mid-air and then began to spin and spin, faster and faster and faster until it became a blur of shining silver.

And then it exploded in a flash of white light.

Luma wiped at her eyes, blinking as the light faded.

'Oh no!' she wailed. 'Where is it? It is

broken? Has it gone?'

'Luma!' Timir called.

Luma looked up.

Timir was sitting still, his mouth closed, and right by his claws was the bracelet, whole and in one piece.

'You can speak again . . . the bracelet!'

Luma picked it up and opened the locket.

'Look,' she said, turning it around to show Timir.

'The flame is purple,' Timir said.

'And it's glowing at last!'

Timir grinned and then jumped on to Luma's lap, nudging his nose into her shoulder. 'I was so afraid,' he said quietly.

'Me too,' Luma said, hugging him tightly. 'But it's stopped now. I think your flame fixed the charm.'

'Luma! Timir!'

'That's Nani,' Luma said. 'Let's go and tell her the good news.'

Luma shuffled out from under the trees.

'We're here, Nani!' she called as they raced through the gate back into Nani's garden.

'Timir.' Nani smiled. 'Your flame has stopped.'

Timir beamed.

'But how?' Nani asked.

'I, um . . . I got a bit angry and

I threw the bracelet,' Luma said. 'And then Timir's flame hit it and it started spinning and spinning and then this giant light exploded out, and look . . .'

Luma passed the bracelet to Nani.

'The flame is glowing,' Nani said. 'But it's purple!'

'What does it mean?' Luma asked. 'And what happens now? Will Timir's flame not come out at all and if it does, will it keep causing chaos?'

'Timir?' Nani said. 'Why don't you try?'

Timir frowned, staring hard at his nostrils. He sucked in a breath and . . .

A teeny burst of flame shot out . . . *purple* flame.

'Ooh,' Luma said.

'Oh my,' Nani gasped.

'Flowers,' Timir said, pointing his claw towards the grass. The daisies that had been ripped out when they had rushed through the garden were firmly planted and swaying in the breeze.

'Do it on me!' Luma said.

'I don't think . . .' Nani began to say.

Timir eagerly let out another burst of purple flame straight at Luma.

Luma's T-shirt and jeans fluttered and a moment later settled the right way round.

'Wow!' Luma said, looking down at herself. 'Do it on Nani!'

'No!' Nani said rather loudly. 'That's all right . . . this is all very strange. The charm is only supposed to turn dragon flame harmless, not purple and definitely not whatever it is doing!'

'Should we test it some more?' Luma asked.

'I think so,' Nani said. 'I would like to know that Timir can control it before sending you two home this evening.'

Chapter Fifteen

'What about the table and chairs?' Luma asked, pointing towards the garden furniture on Nani's patio.

Timir's flame *whished* towards one of the chairs. It lifted in the air, spun exactly once and thumped down.

'Well done, Timir,' Luma said.

'Again!' Timir said, letting out a much bigger burst. The chairs remained still but the large parasol in the middle of the table began to twirl upwards, hovering unsteadily above the table.

'Too much,' Timir said.

'Yes,' Nani agreed, edging towards the parasol as it slowed down to set it right.

'Maybe only use small amounts of flame for the time being.'

'What next?' Luma said, looking around the garden for more things for Timir to practise on. 'I know . . . the lights.'

Luma and Timir ran across the lawn. Small round lights on pointy sticks were stuck into the soil along Nani's flower bed.

'Just try lifting one,' Luma heard Nani call as she walked (rather quickly) towards them.

Timir bent down, shuffling closer to the nearest light.

'*Wooooo*.' He blew out a teeny flame.

The light wobbled.

'A bit more, Timir,' Luma said.

Whoosh!

The light lifted up . . . as did the one next to it and the one next to that.

'Oops,' Timir said.

Luma giggled.

'Ah,' Nani said. 'Better keep practising, Timir. I'll make a start on dinner . . . but I will be watching from the window in case you need me.'

Timir tried again and again and again and soon he knew the exact amount of flame to lift one light or two.

'Now all of them!' Luma said.

Timir let out a long stream of flame. All the lights shot up from the soil, coming together to sway for a moment in the air, before returning neatly to their place.

'Perfect,' Luma said.

Timir spun in a circle. 'More?'

'Hmm,' Luma said. 'What about . . . the trampoline!'

Luma ran through the gate into her garden and climbed on to the trampoline.

Timir eagerly followed, sitting on the edge and blowing flame towards Luma's ankles.

'It tickles!' Luma laughed as she bounced higher than she had ever

bounced before – although not quite as high as in her dream that morning.

'What next?' Timir asked.

'I think the house,' Luma said. 'Your flame did make a lot of mess earlier.'

Luma and Timir sprinted to Nani's house. As soon as they stepped inside the living room, Timir spun in a wide circle, his flame whooshing all around him.

The books slid back on to the bookcase (all except one that flapped about before slamming on to Nani's dresser), the cushions arranged themselves (almost) perfectly on the sofa and the curtains untied and hung mostly as before.

Luma followed Timir into the hallway, grinning as the pictures straightened on the walls and the coats on their pegs unzipped.

And then the doorbell rang.

Chapter Sixteen

'It's me!' Luma heard a voice call.

Luma rushed to the front door and opened it.

'Mum!' She grinned, giving her a big hug.

'Me too!' Timir said, trying to wriggle between them.

'Hello, Timir.' Mum laughed, bending down to pick him up.

'Mum,' Timir cooed, licking the tip of her nose.

'Have you had a good time?' Mum asked, stepping back and opening her arms for Timir to hop down. 'I hope you've both been good for Nani?'

'Err . . . yes.' Luma grinned.

'Woof!' Timir woofed.

Not long after dinner, they left Nani with warm hugs and big waves goodbye and returned home to unpack their overnight bag and get ready for bed.

'I love staying with Nani,' Timir said, snuggling close to Luma as they waited for Mum to come in for their good-night kisses. 'But I love being home too.'

'Yes,' Luma agreed. 'I did miss our bed.'

The door opened and Mum appeared, her hands behind her back.

'What's that?' Luma asked, sitting up and trying to peek round.

'Well, I had a message on the way home

. . . something about your trip to the garden centre being cut short and some unspent pocket money?'

Mum brought her hands forward, revealing two striped paper bags.

'This one is for you, Luma,' Mum said.

Luma opened it and gasped. 'My teddy!' she said, taking it out and hugging the bunny tight.

'And Timir, this is for you.' Mum tipped the bag upside down and out fell a . . .

'Yo-yo!' Timir said, leaping out of the covers to nuzzle it.

'Thank you, Mum.' Luma grinned.

'Good night, my love,' Mum said, bending down to

hug Luma. 'And good night, Timir.' She kissed Timir on his fluffy head.

It took a little while for Luma and Timir to settle after that. Luma couldn't stop hugging her teddy and Timir had leapt off the bed once Mum had left, excited to play with his yo-yo.

Finally, though, as they both began to yawn, Timir climbed up and cuddled next to Luma.

'What a day,' Luma said.

Timir snuffled. 'I never want the hiccups ever again.'

'But now you have your flame,' Luma said.

'Yes,' Timir said.

And then he turned on to his back, opened his mouth and blew softly.

Purple flame danced across the ceiling,

twinkling and glimmering, like a starry night sky.

Luma smiled, her eyes blinking and blinking, until she fell asleep.

The
Prickly Tickle

Chapter One

Luma woke up to a blast of bright light.

She groaned, turning away from her bedside lamp and burrowing under the covers.

'Luma, time to get up now!' she heard Timir call, exactly the same way Mum did when it was school in the morning.

And then the duvet was ripped away and she felt something – or *someone* – clamp on to the bottom of her pyjamas and begin to tug.

'I'm sleeping,' Luma mumbled.

Timir did not listen.

He carried on, pulling Luma's legs out of bed until her toes touched the carpet.

Luma blearily opened her eyes, catching sight of the grey sky through the gap in her curtains. 'Timir! It's still dark outside!'

'It is today,' Timir said.

Luma yawned, too sleepy at first to make sense of what Timir had said, but then . . .

'The dog show!' Luma squealed, leaping up. 'Why didn't you wake me up sooner?'

Timir snorted and then he jumped back on to the bed and began his morning zoomies, crashing into the pillows and sending their favourite zebra teddy spinning on to the carpet.

Luma giggled. She was just as excited as Timir.

Two very long weeks had passed since they'd seen the poster for the show taped

to a fence on one of their walks.

With a little help from Mum and Nani, they had chosen three classes to enter: the agility race, the best trick competition and the fancy dress contest.

Every moment since had been spent practising and practising and practising and now the day had finally arrived!

'We have a lot to do before this afternoon. We need to do our best trick at least ten . . . no, *twenty* times. And you need to work on weaving through the sticks on our agility course and we absolutely, definitely need to tell Nani what spikes to sew on to your costume for the fancy dress . . . I still say a hedgehog would be best.'

Timir stopped. 'Dinosaur.'

'*Hedgehog*,' Luma said.

'Dino—'

'Let's try our best trick,' Luma said, keen to avoid another squabble – the other evening, 'dinosaur' and 'hedgehog' had been nearly all they'd said to one another.

She hopped off the bed and got into the first position.

It had taken quite a bit of deciding to pick which would be the right trick for the competition. Timir had been keen to show off his dancing skills or maybe sneak in a small flame to lift

Luma in the air, but Nani had quickly cautioned them against doing anything that might reveal Timir was not just a dog.

They had eventually settled on Timir jumping over Luma on her hands and knees and then both of them doing three very fast spins, before finishing off with Timir leaping into Luma's arms.

'I'm ready,' Luma called.

Luma felt a whoosh as Timir flew over her. She stood up, ready to do her three spins, when she looked down and realised Timir was not by her side.

Chapter Two

'Timir? Where have you gone?'

Luma heard a muffled groan.

She twirled around, spotting a spiky dragon tail poking out of her pile of teddies.

'Whoops, we forgot,' Luma said, helping a slightly dazed Timir out. 'You always jump too far when you're a dragon.'

Timir did a shake and was soon a fluffy dog.

'Right, now let's . . . ouch!'

'Luma? What is it?' Timir asked.

'I don't know,' Luma said, rubbing her wrist – it was the wrist with the charm bracelet on. 'I think something bit me.'

Timir nosed the bracelet out of the way. 'There is nothing.'

'You're right,' Luma said, turning her arm this way and that. 'No marks or red spots. It must have been a very small bite.'

'A spider?' Timir said.

Luma shivered.

And then she heard a loud, rumbling grumble.

'Timir? Was that your tummy?'

Timir nodded. 'Breakfast?'

'I think we better had,' Luma said. 'You will need lots of energy today.'

'Will there be pancakes with chocolate sauce?' Timir asked.

'Maybe,' Luma said, opening her bedroom door.

Timir woofed and raced ahead.

Luma followed after him, shooting round the corner to find Mum standing at the kitchen counter, stirring a cup of tea.

'Good morning, you two,' Mum said. 'I had a feeling you might be up early today.'

'Yes,' Luma said. 'We have lots of important last-minute practising for this afternoon.'

'Have you told Nani what costume Timir will be wearing?'

'Dinosaur!' Timir said.

'Not yet,' Luma said with a look towards Timir.

'Well, I still think Timir should be a unicorn,' Mum said. 'He would look very handsome with a sparkling horn and rainbow mane.'

'I will *not* be unicorn,' Timir huffed and then he let out a whine. 'Pancakes, Luma?'

'We will decide as soon as Nani is awake,' Luma said. 'Mum, can we . . . err, can *I* have pancakes for breakfast?'

Mum smiled. 'I'll make them for you.'

Luma ran to the living room with a bouncing Timir by her side. It would take Mum at least five minutes to make the pancakes and spread on the chocolate sauce – five minutes they could spend practising!

Chapter Three

'Should we try the best trick again or how about practising our dog show walk?'

Luma did not wait for an answer but rushed off to fetch Timir's harness.

Timir stood very still while Luma slipped it over his head and did up the clips.

'We will walk around the living room,' Luma said, picking up the lead. 'Remember, head high and tail swishing!'

Luma led Timir round the back of the sofa, in front of the telly, by the side of the bookcase and armchair and back to the rug.

'And sit,' Luma said.

Timir sat. 'Now the best trick?'

Luma nodded, quickly taking Timir's harness off and getting down on her hands and knees. 'Ready, steady, go!'

Timir leapt over Luma and raced back to her side.

Luma stood up for their three spins and then opened her arms to catch Timir.

'Excellent,' she said, popping Timir on to the sofa. 'I think we are going to have the most perfect dog show walk and the *best* best trick in the whole dog show!'

'Here you are,' Mum said, walking into the living room. 'One plate of pancakes and one bowl of lovely, yummy *dog* food.'

Timir let out a very loud snort.

'Thanks, Mum,' Luma said, picking up the plate and sitting next to Timir.

Luma waited until she heard Mum's footsteps return to the kitchen and then she ripped one of the pancakes in half and held it out for Timir. 'We do have to share, though,' she said, as he ate the pancake in one gulp and opened his mouth for more.

By the time Timir had snuffled up the

last crumbs, it was almost light outside.

Luma cleared away the remains of their breakfast and rushed back to the living room.

'Time for more practice,' Luma said, sticking her feet in her garden wellies and opening the back door.

Timir whizzed past her, heading straight for their agility course.

The course had taken a whole day to put together and both Mum and Nani had said how much like a real one it was.

They had made jumps out of garden brooms and kitchen mops with flower pots for the stands. Mum had found a plank of old wood and a sturdy, round log in the shed for a see-saw. The weaving poles were made out of long twigs stuck together with sticky tape, along with

Luma's glitter baton and hobby horse.

They'd managed to wedge both of Luma's hula hoops into the sides of bushes and trees for the more challenging jumps.

The edge of the trampoline was the high jump.

And to top it off, they'd lined up the chairs from their garden table and draped an old sheet over to create a tunnel –

although the sheet must have blown off in the wind last night as it was hanging off one of the chairs.

'We will need to fix that,' Luma said. 'Why don't you use your flame, Timir, and I'll check if Nani is awake?'

Luma climbed inside the trampoline and began to bounce, trying to see over the fence into Nani's garden and the back of her house.

* ✹ *

Chapter Four

'No lights on and I can't see Nani,' Luma called.

Timir did not reply. He was too busy concentrating, his flame blowing the sheet high in the air before guiding it down to lie across the chairs.

'Good job, Timir,' Luma said, hopping off the trampoline. 'Let's do a few practice rounds and then we can check again if Nani is awake.'

Luma walked over to the start of the course – the row of broom and mop jumps. 'Timir, are you coming?'

Luma turned around.

Timir was sitting in the same spot, a frown on his face.

'What's wrong?' Luma asked.

'I do not know,' Timir said. 'Something feels funny.'

'Funny how?' Luma asked, walking towards him.

Timir turned to nibble his back. 'Something here,' he said. 'Something prickly and tickly.'

'Let me see,' Luma said, bending down. She softly stroked the space between Timir's little dragon wings. 'Nothing there – maybe you are just a bit itchy?

Or maybe the same thing that bit me has bitten you too?'

Timir stood up and then he shrugged. 'It has gone now. I will do the jumps.'

'If you're sure?' Luma asked.

Timir sprinted off to the start of the course.

Luma hurried to catch up. 'Remember! You have to turn into a dog or you'll be flying over them!'

Timir skidded to a stop and shook.

'Ouch!' Luma cried, staring down at her wrist. 'Something just bit me again too!'

'Luma?'

'What is going on?' Luma scowled, moving the bracelet about, but there were still no marks or anything like a bite.

'*Luma*?'

Luma looked up. 'What is it, Timir?'

'I am dragon,' Timir said. 'I did shake and I am dragon . . . watch.'

Timir shook and . . .

'Ow! It bit me again!'

'Still dragon,' Timir said and then he did another shake.

'Owweee!' Luma screeched, holding her arm close to her chest.

'One more.'

'No! Wait!' Luma said. '**OUCH!**'

Timir went to shake again . . .

'TIMIR, STOP!' Luma shouted. 'I think it's coming from the bracelet or one of the charms . . . not bites, but zaps!'

'What do you mean, Luma?' Timir asked and then he shook one more time.

'**OWWW!**'

Luma quickly slipped the bracelet off, letting it fall on to the damp grass.

The bracelet hopped and danced about.

'Look! It was definitely the bracelet,' Luma said. 'I wonder which charm, though?'

Timir shuffled forward to sniff it. 'It smells all the same.'

Luma carefully picked the bracelet up
and examined each charm in turn. She
couldn't see anything unusual about any
of them. The orb looked the way it always
did. The black and gold dragon was still
black and gold. Luma opened the locket –

the flame inside was purple and sparkly just as it should be.

'It could be the wing charm or the heart?' Luma said. 'We don't know what they do.'

Timir gave the two charms a lick and an extra-long sniff. 'Nothing different.'

'Maybe you should try changing again, but this time I will watch the charms to see which one it is?'

Luma placed the bracelet back on the grass and knelt down beside it.

'I am shaking now,' Timir said.

The bracelet began to jolt and bump about, faster and faster – *too* fast for Luma to see anything but a blur of gold.

'That didn't work,' Luma said. 'I couldn't see anything at all.'

Timir sat down and whined. 'I want

to be a dog and do practising and go to the show.'

'I know,' Luma said, picking up the bracelet and sliding it back on her wrist. 'But it must be trying to tell us something.'

'It is not telling us! It is broken and I will be dragon for ever!'

Timir tipped his head back and wailed.

Chapter Five

'I know! What if we find something that will *make* you turn into a dog?'

Timir sniffled. 'Like what?'

Luma looked around, thinking and thinking, when she caught sight of a bushy tail disappearing among the tall, tall trees at the back of the garden.

'Oooh, look! A squirrel!'

'Squirrel!' Timir roared, charging off.

Luma crossed her fingers – Timir *always* changed into a dog when he chased squirrels as he liked to use his dog woof to shout at them.

She did not, however, hear any barking.

'Did you change?' Luma called.

Timir's head poked out from the leaves, his dragon ears twitching. 'I did not change.'

Luma sighed. 'What else could we try? What can you only do when you're a dog?'

'Chase my fluffy tail?'

'But you need your fluffy dog tail to chase.'

'Dig holes?'

'You can dig holes just as well as a dragon,' Luma said. 'And anyway, you're not allowed after what happened with Mum's flowers.'

Timir flumped down and rolled on to his back.

'I think we had better go and see Nani,' Luma said.

The back door opened and there was Nani in her dressing gown and a beautiful, patterned, black-and-gold shawl wrapped around her shoulders.

'Good morning,' Nani said, hiding a yawn behind her hand. 'I have just woken up.'

'I cannot change,' Timir said, slipping past Nani into the house. 'And I am hungry.'

'Timir,' Luma chided. 'This is not the time to think about food.'

'Can't change?' Nani said. 'What do you mean?'

'Timir is stuck as a dragon,' Luma explained. 'And every time he shakes and tries to change, the bracelet starts zapping

'. . . it was zapping me at first until we realised!'

'Oh my, let's get you inside,' Nani said. 'I think I'm going to need a cup of tea. How about two hot chocolates as well?'

'And a biscuit?' Timir asked, hopping on to the sofa.

Nani chuckled. 'Well, I am glad you haven't lost your appetite.'

Nani disappeared into the kitchen and soon they heard the sound of the kettle rumbling.

'I hope Nani knows what to do,' Luma said. 'I will be upset for ever if we can't go to the show.'

And then Timir jumped.

'Timir? Are you all right?' Luma asked.

'Prickly,' Timir murmured, bending round to nibble his back. 'And tickly.'

'Like before?' Luma asked. 'Should I scratch you? I might not have been bitten but maybe you actually were!'

Luma ran her hands up and down Timir's back.

'Get that itch!' Timir said, swaying side to side and letting out a dragon purr.

'What is happening here?' Nani asked, her hands full of cups and a small plate with two biscuits balanced on top.

'Timir is itchy,' Luma said.

'A prickly tickle,' Timir said and then he tilted his head. 'Wait . . . it has stopped again.'

Nani placed the cups and plate on the table. 'Hmm, an itchy back,' she said. 'And Timir can't change into a dog?'

'Yes,' Luma said. 'What are we going to do? We will have to leave for the show in a few hours and if Timir is a dragon, we won't be able to go!'

Timir – his mouth full of biscuit – let out a sad howl. 'I want to go, Nani! I want to do jumps and show-dog walking and our trick and be a dinosaur!'

'Ah,' Nani said. 'You have decided on Timir's costume, then?'

'No, we have not,' Luma said. 'But we won't need a costume at all if we can't work out what is wrong with him!'

'I think you two should have another

play in the garden,' Nani said. 'Maybe practise going round your agility course or have a bounce on the trampoline.'

'But—' Luma said.

'Maybe if you're not concentrating too much on the problem you might find the answer.'

Luma frowned. 'What could the answer be?'

Nani smiled. 'Finish your drinks. I am going to get myself dressed and I will come out shortly to see you both.'

Chapter Six

Luma and Timir quickly drank their hot chocolates and went back outside.

'What should we do now?' Luma asked Timir as he trotted to the gate that separated Nani's garden from theirs.

'I want to do the course,' Timir said.

'Yes, I suppose we should practise like Nani said . . . especially the weaving poles.'

Timir did a little whine. He really did not like the weaving poles. Going in and out so fast made him feel very dizzy.

'I will start from the beginning,' he said, heading to the brooms and mops.

Timir set off, doing little hops over

the first three jumps and then he sped up towards the see-saw.

'Slow down!' Luma called, running beside him – Timir had wobbled off several times before.

Timir nodded, carefully shuffling on to the plank of wood until it tipped forward. He swayed once and then was tiptoeing down the other side.

'Well done!' Luma cheered. 'Now for the hula hoops.'

Timir bounded ahead, jumping through the first glitter hoop and leaping through the next.

'Tunnel next,' Luma said, trying to keep up.

Timir picked up speed, shooting under the sheet and . . .

'Timir? Where are you?' Luma ran to the other end.

'I got that prickly tickle,' she heard Timir call.

Luma knelt down and crawled inside the sheet tunnel.

Timir was all twisted up trying to bite his back. 'I cannot get it!'

'I will scratch it for you, but I think it would be best to get out of the tunnel first.'

Timir followed Luma as she shuffled backwards – or tried to. Every few seconds he had to stop and spin around, desperate to get the prickly tickle.

Luma had to reach back in and pull him out.

'Itchy right there,' Timir said, nosing under his wing.

Luma scratched hard up and down.

'More left,' Timir said.

Luma scratched to the left.

'And right,' Timir said. 'And up . . . and down . . . and left again!'

Luma rubbed him all over with both hands.

'Stop!' Timir said.

Luma lifted her hands off Timir's back.

'Yes.' He nodded. 'Prickly tickle has all gone now.'

'How odd,' Luma said. 'Itches from bites don't usually stop and start that way. I wonder if it is something else?'

Timir, however, did not seem as concerned as Luma. He zoomed in a circle and then galloped off towards the trampoline. 'I do the high jump!'

'Maybe we should go back to Nani?'

Luma called after him.

But Timir was already crouching down, ready to spring upwards.

And then something very strange happened.

Timir's wings, which had only ever fluttered before, began to swoop up and down, and soon, Timir was not jumping, but flying!

Chapter Seven

'Ahhh!' Timir flew straight past the trampoline and landed in a bush.

'Timir!' Luma raced towards him.

'My wings . . . they flew!' Timir cried as he scrambled out.

'They did, Timir!' Luma said. 'I think they've grown as well.'

Timir twisted around, trying to see. 'And they feel funny.'

'Prickly and tickly again?' Luma asked and then she gasped. 'Of course! It all makes sense . . . the zaps and your itch and not being able to change into a dog.'

'What makes sense?' Timir asked.

'It must have been the wing charm

all along,' Luma continued with a grin. 'Timir . . . I think it's time for you to learn to fly!'

Timir tilted his head right back to look at the sky. A flock of birds passed over, diving and ducking, before moving out of sight.

'I am not sure I want to fly,' he said quietly. 'It looks too far away and you will not be there.'

'But, Timir, flying is amazing,' Luma said. 'I wish I could fly.'

'You do?' Timir said.

'Oh, yes! Soaring in the clouds and flying wherever I want. It would be so much fun.'

Timir did not look at all convinced.

'You don't have to fly too far if you don't want to,' Luma said. 'And I bet once you have flown about for a bit, you will be able to turn into a dog again.'

'We can go to the show?' Timir said.

'Exactly,' Luma said.

Timir sighed. 'I will learn, but . . . how, Luma?'

'Hmm,' Luma said. 'What if I put you on the edge of the trampoline and then you try and fly down?'

Timir gave a hesitant nod.

Luma lifted Timir up and settled him on the edge.

Timir stayed completely still.

'How about just moving your wings for a bit?' Luma suggested.

Timir flapped them up and down.

'Good,' Luma said. 'Now try jumping and moving your wings at the same time.'

Timir jumped, his wings moving

slowly at first and then he jumped a little higher and his wings took over, lifting him upwards.

'Luma! I am doing it!'

'You are, Timir!' Luma called. 'You are flying!'

Timir was almost smiling as he flew about but his smile soon turned to fright.

'What's happening?' Luma shouted.

Timir began to zigzag, shooting left and then right, his wings beating wildly as he lost control and tumbled straight back into the same bush he crashed into before.

'I did not like flying,' Timir snuffled as he came out, leaves stuck to his horns.

'You were doing so well, though,' Luma said. 'You just need to practise some more. Remember when we first set up our agility course? You knocked over

all the jumps and now you can do the whole course perfectly.'

Timir shook his head.

'Well . . . maybe that was enough flying for today?' Luma said. 'You could try changing into a dog?'

Timir quickly nodded.

'I think I will take off the bracelet first,' Luma said. 'I don't want to get zapped again.'

Timir waited until Luma had put the bracelet safely on the grass and then he did a big shake.

'There!' Luma cried. 'I see your fluffy fur and your dog nose.'

But his fur and nose soon faded and Timir was all dragon again.

Timir tried once more.

This time he did not change at all and the bracelet jumped about frantically on the grass.

Timir gulped.

Chapter Eight

Luma picked Timir up and put him back on the edge of the trampoline.

'Are you ready?' Luma asked.

Timir did a little hop, but his wings remained at his side. 'I am afraid,' he snuffled.

Luma was quiet for a moment. 'Timir? We don't have to go to the dog show,' she said. 'If you're not ready to learn to fly, then we can stay at home. I'm sure Nani will be able to help if we do.'

'Oh, no, Luma.' Timir frowned. 'I want to go.'

'But—'

Timir stood up straight and puffed out his chest. 'I *can* do it.'

And then he hunched down, his wings lying low and, with an enormous flap, he lifted up into the air, higher and higher, until he was flying round the garden.

Luma cheered as Timir swooped over the mops and brooms, shot past the hula hoops and . . .

'Timir! Watch out for the—'

Timir's tail and back claws caught the edge of their chair tunnel. He yelped as he flew on, the sheet flapping behind.

Luma sprinted towards him and just managed to grab hold of it before Timir swerved to avoid the fence.

'Luma!' Timir shouted as he spiralled sharply upwards before plummeting right back down and – very luckily – landing right in the middle of the trampoline.

Luma winced as he bounced up and down. She quickly jumped on to the trampoline and crawled through the net to his side.

'Are you all right? Are you hurt?'

Timir shook his head. 'I need to go higher. There is too much in the way.'

'Higher?' Luma said. 'I'm not sure that's a good idea. What if you lose control again? You could end up anywhere.'

'I will do it, Luma,' Timir said. 'And then I can change into a dog and we can go to the show.'

'Timir, please! Don't . . .'

But it was too late.

Timir was already on the edge and then he was off, soaring towards the sky, his wings beating fast behind him, until he became a shimmery blur in the distance.

Luma tried to be patient.

Timir would come back any second, she just knew it.

She sat down on one of the chairs from their tunnel to wait, but she couldn't help letting out a worried sigh. She couldn't see any sign of Timir anywhere.

She did, however, catch a glimpse of something flashing in the grass.

Luma went to investigate.

'Oh, the charm bracelet,' Luma said, picking it up from where she had left it when Timir had last tried to change into a dog.

She was about to slip it back on to her wrist, when she saw the flash again.

'What?' She frowned and then . . . 'Of course! The dragon charm!'

The charm had helped her find Timir when they both got lost in the park during the puppy training lesson, its flashes telling her whether he was close or far.

Luma held up the bracelet to see the little dragon charm and there . . . a flash of soft light! She watched for another, counting out loud. 'One, two, three . . . twenty, another flash!'

She counted again, this time getting all the way to thirty and then again, all the way to forty and then a whole minute passed before the dragon charm lit up.

'No, Timir,' Luma said. 'You're going too far away.'

Luma felt a tear slip down her cheek. What if Timir really had got lost? What if he still couldn't control his wings and was stuck somewhere and needed help?'

Luma stood up and ran to Nani's back door.

Chapter Nine

'Luma? Is everything all right? Where is Timir?'

'Timir can fly and he's . . . he's gone!' Luma managed to get out before bursting into tears.

'My Luma,' Nani said, bundling Luma into her arms and hugging her tight. 'Let's get you a tissue and you can tell me what has happened.'

Luma sat on the sofa, wiped her eyes and began to explain.

'Ah,' Nani said. 'I thought that may be what it was . . . flying! My goodness!'

'But, Nani,' Luma said. 'Timir could barely control his wings and he was very scared. He only went higher because I said maybe if he flew more he would be able to turn into a dog again so we could go to the show!'

'Don't worry, my love,' Nani said. 'I'm sure Timir will master his wings in no time.'

'What if he gets lost?'

'Dragons have an excellent sense of direction. He will find his way home.'

Luma's shoulders dropped. She wanted Timir safely back with her right now. She held up the bracelet to check the dragon charm again when she noticed something a little odd.

'Nani?' Luma asked. 'Does the wing charm look brighter to you?'

Nani peered at the bracelet and smiled. 'It does indeed.'

'What does that mean?' Luma asked.

'It means, little one,' Nani said, 'Timir has learnt to control his wings.'

Luma jumped up. 'And he'll be back soon?'

'I believe so,' Nani said. 'Now, I need to return to the very important task of finishing Timir's costume, otherwise it won't be ready in time.'

'But we never told you whether we wanted Timir to be a hedgehog or a dinosaur?'

'Not to worry,' Nani said. 'I have made my own decision.'

Luma tried not to frown. She still very much wanted Timir to be a spiky hedgehog.

'Off you go and I will see you at the show.'

Luma returned to the garden, nearly tripping over her feet as she stared at the sky, hoping for a glimpse of Timir coming home.

'Luma? *Luma!*'

'He's back . . . Timir!'

Chapter Ten

Luma dashed through the gate and into their garden.

'Timir! Where are you?'

And then she saw him – or a blur in the shape of a dragon as Timir galloped towards her and nearly sent her flying as he jumped into her arms.

Luma held him tightly. 'I was very worried.'

Timir nuzzled her cheek and gave her a little lick. 'I am here.'

'I'm so glad you're home,' Luma said. 'But what happened? Where did you go?'

Timir hopped out of her arms.

'Watch,' he said and then he flapped his wings.

'Oh!' Luma gasped. 'They're beautiful!'

Timir's wings were now twice as long as they had been before, shimmering with hints of purple and blue and sparkling silver and gold.

Timir leapt into the air, his new wings carrying him upwards as he twirled and rolled, before diving back towards Luma.

'And you can fly so well!'

'My wings did not listen at first,' Timir said, settling back on the ground. 'But the more I flew the better it was until I flew so high I was in the clouds . . . they are not fluffy like you said, Luma, they are wet!'

Luma giggled. 'Where else?'

'I flew to the park with the playground and I sat on the highest branch of the tallest tree and I could see everywhere!'

'Wow!' Luma smiled. 'I wish I could fly with you.'

'Me too . . . Luma?'

'Yes, Timir?'

'Is it time for lunch?'

Luma laughed. 'I think it might be. Should we go inside and . . . wait! Can you change into a dog now?'

Timir frowned. 'I do not know.'

'Let me take the bracelet off,' Luma said. 'Just in case.'

Timir did a ginormous shake and . . .

'Yay! You did it,' Luma cried. 'You're a dog!'

'Woof!' Timir woofed.

'Luma? Timir?'

Mum was standing in the back doorway. 'Time for lunch.'

'Phew!' Luma said. 'That was good timing.'

'And after lunch we can go to the show!' Timir cheered.

Chapter Eleven

Luma fed Timir his half of her cheese toastie, cucumber and carrot sticks as he sat by her legs under the kitchen table.

'Mm, crunchy,' Timir said, nibbling on the last carrot.

'Mum?' Luma asked. 'How long until we leave?'

Mum smiled. 'Actually, it's time to get ready now.'

Luma sat in the car with Timir on her lap and soon they were driving into a big open field where the show was taking place.

There were dogs everywhere, big and small, wide and slim, fluffy and curly, some woofing, some howling, some hiding in arms and some tugging on the ends of leads.

Timir wove in and out of Luma's feet as they followed Mum to the desk with a huge *ENTER HERE!* banner overhead.

Mum signed their names up for their three classes and Luma received a small

rectangle of paper with the number 589 on it and a safety pin to attach it to her T-shirt.

'Look!' Timir said. 'Reyansh and Arjun.'

'Oh, yes,' Luma said. 'But Nani isn't with them?'

'Timir!' Reyansh shouted, breaking away from Auntie and Arjun to run towards them.

'Reyansh!' Timir called, tugging towards him.

Reyansh skidded to a stop and knelt down to scratch Timir's fluffy ears. 'Who's a good boy,' he said.

'I'm a good boy,' Timir said, wagging his tail.

'Luma, are you excited?' Auntie asked, giving her a big hug.

'Yes, although . . .' Luma looked around.

The show was very busy and she was beginning to feel quite nervous, and where *was* Nani?

Then they heard an announcement over the loud speaker.

'All competitors for the beginners' agility class, please make your way to ring one.'

'That's you,' Mum said.

Luma was only half listening. She was still searching the sea of people and dogs for Nani.

'Do you think Nani will be here in time?' she asked Mum.

'I don't know,' Mum said. 'She was very busy finishing Timir's costume, but I'm sure she'll be here as soon as she can.'

Luma and Timir, Mum, Auntie and the boys walked over to the agility course.

There was a large map of the jumps and obstacles pinned to the fence with arrows showing which way to go round.

Luma studied it and gulped. 'It seems a bit harder than our course at home . . . and longer,' she said quietly to Timir.

'I will do it,' Timir said, although he didn't look quite sure either as he stared at the dreaded line of weaving poles, double the amount of their own.

They watched the other competitors zoom round the course, and all too soon a voice called, 'Number 589!'

Chapter Twelve

'Good luck, Luma,' Mum said as Luma and Timir entered the ring.

'Nani's still not here,' Luma said to Timir as they walked to the start.

'Nani *is* here,' Timir said. 'Right over there.'

Luma grinned as she watched Nani make her way towards the ring and then Nani saw them and waved.

Luma very happily waved back.

'What is Nani holding in the big bag?' Timir asked.

'I think it's your costume,' Luma said.

'Ooh, dinosaur,' Timir said.

'Maybe, and now we need to concentrate,' Luma said, seeing a man with a whistle and a stopwatch enter the ring.

There was a sharp blast and . . . 'Ready and go!'

Timir flew over the first jump, and then the second and the third.

He dashed through the tunnel, spinning in a circle as he came out the other side.

'Wheeee!' he cried.

Luma giggled, running alongside him.

Timir ran up the side of the see-saw – a much larger see-saw than the one they'd made at home. He wobbled in the middle as the plank tipped, his paw slipping . . .

Luma held her breath.

Timir shot forward and trotted safely down the other side.

'Keep going, Timir!' Luma called.

He flew over another jump, through a hula hoop and then it was time for the weaving poles.

In. Out. In. Out. In. Out.

'You can do it, Timir!'

'Missed one,' Timir said, turning around and trying again.

'Yay!' Luma shouted as he wove around the last pole and galloped ahead and then Timir was soaring over the last jump and thumping to a sit on top of the square platform that marked the finish line.

'Good round!' the man with the whistle and the stopwatch called.

There were claps and cheers, none bigger than from Mum, Nani, Auntie and her cousins.

'Very well done, Luma,' Mum called. 'And what an amazing job, Timir!'

'The best boy,' Reyansh said.

'You were brilliant,' Arjun said, with a slightly reluctant smile.

'I got it all on here!' Auntie said, tapping her phone.

'I am so very proud of you both,' Nani said.

'What is in the bag, Nani?' Timir asked.
'Am I a dinosaur?'

'No.' Nani bent down to answer Timir.

'Is Timir a hedgehog?'

Nani shook her head.

'Am I a . . . *unicorn*?' Timir scowled.

Nani chuckled. 'Never.'

And then the man with the stopwatch called out to the crowd, 'Well done to all competitors! We now have our top five! Contestants 895, 213, 519, 645 and 589, please enter the ring!'

'That's our number!' Luma gasped.

Luma led Timir inside and lined up with the four other owners and their dogs.

'First place to 213,' the man said, passing a lady and her large fluffy dog a bright red rosette.

'Second place to 645,' the man

continued, handing a blue rosette to a man and his tall, slim dog.

'And third place to . . . 589!'

Chapter Thirteen

Luma beamed as the man gave her a yellow rosette with *Third Place* in gold letters on it.

'We did it, Timir!'

Timir spun in bouncy circles.

After more hugs and congratulations, Mum told them it was almost time for the best trick class.

Luma and Nani trailed behind Mum, Auntie and Arjun – Reyansh was very proudly leading Timir.

'I am very glad Timir made it back in time,' Nani said.

'His wings have grown too,' Luma said. 'I can't wait for you to see them.'

'Me too.' Nani chuckled.

Luma left Nani behind, collected Timir from Reyansh and entered the ring alongside five other competitors.

She felt a lot less nervous this time after their success in the agility course.

They watched a dog high five its owner, another twirl and hop on its back legs and one dog howl on command – all the other dogs, inside and outside

the ring, including Timir, joined in. The
pair next to them did a trick similar to
their own, with a small, fluffy dog
jumping through its owner's arms.

Lastly, it was Luma and Timir's turn.
Luma got on to her hands and knees.
'Alright, Timir, let's do it!'
Timir soared over Luma.
They did their three spins and then

Luma held out her arms and Timir jumped . . . a little too hard, crashing into Luma's chest and knocking her right over.

'Whoops!' Luma said, quickly scrambling back to her feet, a sheepish Timir at her side.

They were given a green fourth-place rosette and just as many cheers from their family.

Finally, it was time to get ready for the fancy dress competition.

Mum, Auntie and the boys went ahead to get cups of tea and snacks and Nani led Luma and Timir to a quiet corner.

'What am I?' Timir asked, hopping all about.

Nani put the bag on the ground and pulled out a shimmering, scaly costume. 'I thought, after this morning, Timir, you should be a . . .'

'Dragon!' Luma grinned.

'Yes,' Nani said. 'Now, stand still, Timir.'

Nani was just about to slip the costume over Timir's head when a loud, worried voice came booming over the speakers dotted around the showground.

'We have a lost puppy! A LOST PUPPY! Please could everyone keep their eyes peeled for Maisie, a small, white and tan dog, with a pink collar and lead. Maisie was last seen running in the direction of the trees!'

There were gasps and murmurs from

the crowd and more than a few people turned and hurried towards the trees at the edge of the show ring to help.

'Oh my,' Nani said. 'A lost puppy!'

'She must be so afraid and these fields are so big,' Luma said. 'The puppy could be anywhere!'

'Nani? Put it on!' Timir said, jumping up and tugging on the costume.

'But, Timir?' Luma said. 'Don't you think we should help? Remember when we got lost in the forest after you chased the squirrel at the dog training class?'

Timir shuddered. 'I did not like the woods and the forest at all.'

And then Luma had an idea. 'Timir! You could *fly* above the trees. I bet you would spot the puppy in no time!'

* ✱ *

Chapter Fourteen

Timir whined, turning to the ring where the other fancy dress competitiors were beginning to line up. 'My costume, Luma and . . . and my dog show walk?'

'I know,' Luma said. 'But we might be the puppy's only chance.'

Timir let out a small sigh and then nodded. 'You are right. We will find her.'

'What a very kind choice to make.' Nani smiled. 'But be careful not to be seen, Timir.'

Luma caught a flash of Mum, Auntie and the boys' puzzled faces as she and Timir sprinted past them to the trees.

They found a quiet corner away from the calls for the lost puppy for Timir to change.

'I know you can find her, Timir,' Luma

said. 'And if you go too far, I will use the dragon charm to find you.'

Timir flapped his wings and took off, soaring towards the nearest high branch, and hiding himself between the thick leaves.

Luma watched as Timir flew from tree to tree and then all of a sudden he dove out of sight.

Luma ran to where she saw Timir disappear, pushing through twigs and branches, until she stepped out on to a small clearing.

Timir was hunched down at one end and there, huddled by the trunk of a tree, was the lost puppy!

'Maisie?' Luma called softly.

The puppy shivered and cried.

Luma slowly stepped closer and closer

until she could reach down and grab
Maisie's lead.

'We found you!' Luma grinned, picking
the puppy up. The puppy gave her a giant
lick. 'Come on, Timir,' Luma said. 'Let's go.'

Luma carried the puppy with Timir
trotting proudly at her side all the way
through the trees and back to the show
ground.

Right near the stand with the ENTER HERE banner, a lady was sitting on a stool, a clump of tissues in her hand as she stared sadly into the distance.

'I think that's your owner,' Luma said to Maisie.

Maisie yapped and wiggled in her arms.

'Oh, my darling!' the lady cried, jumping up as she saw them.

The puppy leapt into the lady's arms.

'Thank you so very much,' the lady said, wiping away a tear. 'I thought she was lost for ever!'

'It was my dog, Timir. He found her in the trees,' Luma said.

'What a clever boy.' The lady grinned.

Timir spun in a circle and woofed.

Chapter Fifteen

Luma and Timir returned to their family waiting by the side of the ring.

'Luma? What happened?' Mum asked. 'Nani said you went to search for the lost puppy.'

'We did,' Luma said. 'And . . . we found her!'

'But you missed the competition.' Arjun frowned. 'A huge dog dressed up as a bumblebee won.'

Timir whined, his ears drooping.

'What if Timir wears his costume now?' Nani said.

Nani took the costume out of the bag once more and put it on Timir.

He didn't look quite like he did when

he was a real dragon – tufts of his fluffy dog fur could be seen poking out around the edges, but it was a very close match.

'Timir! You're a dragon,' Reyansh cried.

'The best, most kindest dragon,' Luma said, bending down to hug him.

And then the voice from before came booming back over the speakers.

'Could competitor 589 please enter Ring One!'

'That's us,' Luma said.

'And this is Ring One,' Nani said.

'Look, there is one of the judges inside,' Mum said. 'You had better go and see.'

Luma hesitantly led Timir into the ring. It was completely empty other than the judge, but there was still quite a crowd of spectactors round the edges.

As Luma and Timir walked towards the middle, the judge held up his megaphone.

'Ladies and gentlemen, we have here the finders of the lost puppy!'

The crowd began to clap and cheer.

'What are your names?' the judge asked Luma.

'Luma,' Luma said. 'And this is Timir.'

The judge smiled and spoke through

the megaphone again. 'As a thank you to Luma and Timir for their help, we would like to present them with a special prize.'

The judge passed Luma a bag of dog treats, a squeaky squirrel toy and, best of all, a large red rosette. In the middle, someone had written in big gold letters: *Best Finders!*

'Why don't you take a lap around the ring?' the judge suggested as the cheers and claps grew louder.

'I will do my dog show walk,' Timir said, setting off. 'Head high and tail swishing!'

Luma giggled and skipped to catch up.

Chapter Sixteen

They spent another hour or two at the dog show, watching the other competitions, races and classes, eating ice cream and browsing the stalls full of everything you would ever need for a dog and then finally it was time to go home.

Luma arranged their three rosettes on the shelf in her bedroom next to her music box.

'What do you think?' Luma asked, standing back to look at them.

Timir dropped his new squeaky squirrel and hopped on to the bed. He nudged their special red rosette with his nose. 'Now it is perfect.'

Luma turned to him and grinned. 'It was a very good thing you learnt to fly this morning,' she said. 'Without your wings, we would never have found the lost puppy.'

Timir beamed. 'I do some more flying,' he said, shaking and changing into a dragon.

'I think you will have to take your costume off first,' Luma said, as his horns and wings tried to poke through the scaly fabric.

'Oh,' Timir said, doing another shake back into a dog. 'No.'

In fact, Timir remained in his dragon

costume all through dinner, Luma's bath and Mum putting them to bed (Mum did try to take it off but Timir hid in Luma's teddy pile).

'I really think you should take it off now,' Luma said, snuggling under the duvet. 'It won't be very comfortable to sleep in.'

Timir sighed. 'But I do not want to, Luma.'

'You can put it back on tomorrow,' Luma said.

Timir grinned, finally wiggling out of the costume.

By the time he jumped on to the bed, he was a real dragon once more.

Luma lifted up the duvet so Timir could get in.

A second later, however, his head

popped out. 'I am not feeling sleepy. I am too excited still.'

Luma giggled. 'It has been a very exciting day . . . how about a story?'

'What sort of story?' Timir asked, cuddling into Luma and resting his head on her chest.

'Hmm,' Luma said, thinking. 'Once upon a time, there was a little dragon—'

'I am not that little,' Timir interrupted. 'I am quite big, I think.'

'Once upon a time, there was a . . . *medium*-sized dragon.'

'Good.' Timir yawned. 'Go on.'

'And one day he woke up with a prickly tickly itch on his back . . .'

LOOK OUT FOR

LUMA

and the

GRUMPY
DRAGON